D1219583

Ned Loses His Head

by David Michael Slater
illustrated by S.G. Brooks

For Zach, Molly, Naava & Max—DMS

visit us at
www.abdopublishing.com

Published by Red Wagon, a division of the ABDO Publishing Group, 8000 West 78th Street, Edina, Minnesota, 55439. Copyright © 2008 by Abdo Consulting Group, Inc. International copyrights reserved in all countries. All rights reserved. No part of this book may be reproduced in any form without written permission from the publisher. Looking Glass Library™ is a trademark and logo of Red Wagon.

Printed in the United States.

Text by David Michael Slater
Illustrations by S.G. Brooks
Edited by Stephanie Hedlund
Interior layout and design by Becky Daum
Cover design by Becky Daum

Library of Congress Cataloging-in-Publication Data

Slater, David Michael.
    Ned loses his head / David Michael Slater ; illustrated by S.G. Brooks.
        p. cm.
    Summary: After his mother tells him that he would "lose his head if not attached," Ned dreams he does just that and the problems it causes.
    ISBN 978-1-60270-011-6
    [1. Body, Human--Fiction. 2. English language--Idioms--Fiction. 3. Figures of speech--Fiction. 4. Humorous stories.] I. Brooks, S. G., ill. II. Title.
    PZ7.S62898Ne 2007
    [E]--dc22
                            2007003795

"NED!

YOU'D LOSE YOUR HEAD IF IT WASN'T ATTACHED!"

Ned's headstrong mom was working up a head of steam. He'd headed home without his headband, his headphones, and his headgear—again. The only thing he had was a horrible headache.

"HEAD UP TO YOUR ROOM RIGHT THIS INSTANT YOUNG MAN!"

Ned dove headfirst onto his bed, and banged on the headboard until he fell asleep. He dreamt about turning people's heads, but the only head he was turning was his own,

over

and over

and over.

Finally, it popped off his neck,

fell off the bed

and headed right through the door.

Ned got up feeling lightheaded, so
he headed to the bathroom to clear
his head. He made no headway at
this, of course. He *had* no head!

Ned was terrified—he could just
imagine the headlines...

Ned tried to keep his head about him, but it was a little late for that. He wandered around his room in circles, unable to make heads or tails of the situation.

By accident, he headed out of his room. He tripped on a laundry basket sitting at the head of the stairs and tumbled headless over heels all the way down.

Ned's mom looked out from the kitchen where she was cutting up a head of lettuce for her headcheese salad. Getting a head start on dinner helps any head of household keep her head above water.

"Why, thanks Ned!" she said, surprised.

"That's using your head!"

Ned headed to the laundry room and set down the basket. He had to think like a headhunter, but it was hard with no head.

Ned was upset. He wanted to put his head in his hands, but he couldn't do that until he got his hands on his head!

A few minutes later, Ned's cat Hedwig came in. He eyed Ned's head and then headed straight for it.

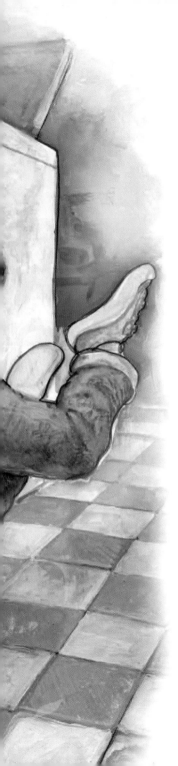

Ned felt something being dragged over his feet.
Hedwig was heading for the kitty door with
his head!

Ned leapt after Hedwig, trying to head him off.
But the rascal slipped through the tiny door just
ahead of him. Ned tried to head through after
Hedwig, but he didn't fit.

"Where is your head, young man?!"

Ned's mom found him trying to fit through the cat door.
But then she said, "Did Hedwig take my headscarf again?"

She shook her head and headed off.

Ned stumbled through the back door and headed toward the garden where Hedwig buried the birds he caught.

He tripped on Hedwig and took a header into the Big-Head Clovers, and there it was—**his head!**

Ned held his head high and tried to put it on his neck, but something yanked it away.

Birds!

There were Black-headed Grosbeaks, Yellow-headed Blackbirds, Brown-headed Cowbirds, White-headed Woodpeckers, and Loggerhead Shrikes!

The birds carried Ned's head up toward the
thunderheads above. For the first time, Ned's head
really was in the clouds. Then they headed down to
their usual spot next to the chimney. Hedwig hissed
at them.

"Weeding too??!"
Ned's mom called through the window. She was left scratching her head. Then she said,

**"I think someone deserves a big fat kiss on the forehead!
Heads up, here I come!"**

The back door slammed shut behind her. Ned felt the vibrations like a headwind from all the way across the yard. He knew his mother was heading right for him. Events were finally coming to a head.

Ned got to his feet and pulled his shirt up to hide his headlessness. When his mom reached him, he hugged her, pretending to put himself in a headlock. But Hedwig slipped between them and Ned accidentally stomped on his tail. Hedwig screamed and jumped on Ned's mom's head. She threw him headlong into the air.

Hedwig landed on the roof and charged head first at the birds. The birds got a head start though, and flew away, leaving Ned's head behind. That really sent Ned's head spinning. It rolled down the roof and out over the yard on a telephone wire. It was just over headless Ned when it fell.

"NED!"

Ned's mom cried, waking him up. She planted a huge kiss on his forehead. "I'm sorry I shouted at you earlier," she said. "I guess I just lost my head for a moment."

"That's okay, Mom," said Ned with a sigh. "It happens even to the headiest people sometimes."

Ned's mom's eyes shone like headlights. "You've got a good head on your shoulders, Ned," she said. "I mean it, head and shoulders above the rest."

"I know," said Ned. "But don't worry, I won't let it go to my head."

READING COMPREHENSION QUESTIONS

1. What did Ned forget to bring home with him?

2. What is the name of Ned's cat?

3. How did Ned's head get outside?

4. Where is Ned's head carried to?

5. What does Ned imagine his head will do next?

ABOUT THE AUTHOR

David Michael Slater lives and teaches seventh grade Language Arts in Portland, Oregon. He uses his talents to educate and entertain with his humorous books and informative presentations. David writes for children, young adults, and adults. Some of his other titles include *Cheese Louise*, *The Ring Bear* (an SSLI-Honor Book), and *Jacques & Spock* (a Children's Book-of-the-Month Alternate Selection). More information about David and his books can be found at **www.abdopublishing.com**.